FAVORITE
BASEBALL
★ TEAMS ★

CHICAGO
CUBS

BY K. C. KELLEY

Published by The Child's World®
1980 Lookout Drive • Mankato, MN 56003-1705
800-599-READ • www.childsworld.com

ACKNOWLEDGMENTS
The Child's World®: Mary Berendes,
    Publishing Director
The Design Lab: Kathleen Petelinsek, Design
Shoreline Publishing Group, LLC: James
    Buckley Jr., Production Director

PHOTOS
Cover: Focus on Baseball
Interior: All by Focus on Baseball except: AP/Wide
World: 18, 22 (2).

LIBRARY OF CONGRESS
CATALOGING-IN-PUBLICATION DATA
Kelley, K. C.
  Chicago Cubs / by K. C. Kelley.
    p. cm. — (Favorite baseball teams)
  Includes index.
  ISBN 978-1-60253-377-6 (library bound : alk.
paper)
  1. Chicago Cubs (Baseball team)—History—
Juvenile literature. 2. Baseball—Illinois—Chicago—
History—Juvenile literature. I. Title. II. Series.
  GV875.C58K45 2010
  796.357'640977311—dc22   2009041219

Printed in the United States of America
Mankato, Minnesota
November 2009
F11460

On the cover:
Alfonso Soriano, Outfield

CONTENTS

Go, Cubs!

Chicago is sometimes called the "Second City." That's where the Cubs have been for more than one-hundred years. That's how long it's been since the team won a **World Series**. Ouch! However, their fans remain **loyal** and loud. The "Cubbies" are among baseball's best-loved teams. Let's meet the Cubs!

Cubs win! Cubs win! High-fives and smiles for the Cubbies! ▶

Who Are the Cubs?

The Chicago Cubs are a team in baseball's National League (N.L.). The N.L. joins with the American League to form Major League Baseball. The Cubs play in the Central Division of the N.L. The division winners get to play in the league playoffs. The playoff winners from the two leagues face off in the World Series. The Cubs have won two World Series championships.

◀ Safe! A great slide by this Cubs player knocked the ball out of the third baseman's glove.

Where They Came From

The Chicago Cubs haven't always been the Cubs. The N.L. had its first season in 1876. The Chicago White Stockings played in that first N.L. season. They became the Colts in 1890, then the Orphans in 1898. Finally, in 1903, they got their current name. The Cubs have always played in Chicago. They have been in their current ballpark longer than any other N.L. team.

Check out the old-style baggy uniforms on these Cubs players from 1932. ▶

Who They Play

The Chicago Cubs play 162 games each season. That includes about 15 games against the other teams in their division, the N.L. Central. The Cubs have won three N.L. Central championships. The other Central teams are the Cincinnati Reds, the Houston Astros, the Milwaukee Brewers, the Pittsburgh Pirates, and the St. Louis Cardinals. The Cubs and the Cardinals are big **rivals**. Their games always get the fans charged up! The Cubbies also play some teams from the American League. Their A.L. **opponents** change every year.

◀ Up, up, and away goes this Cubs second baseman. He just forced out the sliding Cardinals runner.

Where They Play

Wrigley Field has been the home of the Cubs since 1916. It is the oldest ballpark in the N.L. Many of the walls are made of brick. The **outfield** fence is covered with bright green ivy plants! Some buildings are very close to Wrigley Field. Fans can sit on their roofs to watch the game! The area around the beloved ballpark is fun on game days. It's called "Wrigleyville." The ballpark was the last in the Majors to get lights for night baseball. Until 1988, all Cubs home games were day games!

This famous lighted sign shines over the main entrance to Wrigley Field. ▶

WRIGLEY FIELD
HOME OF
CHICAGO CUBS
WELCOME TO
WRIGLEY FIELD

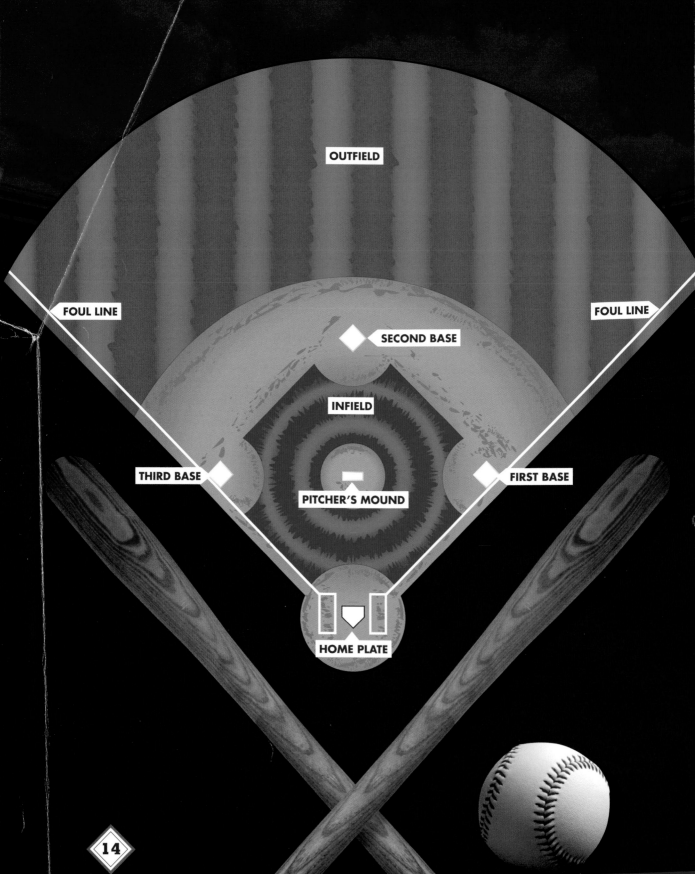

OUTFIELD

FOUL LINE

FOUL LINE

SECOND BASE

INFIELD

THIRD BASE

FIRST BASE

PITCHER'S MOUND

HOME PLATE

The Baseball Diamond

Baseball games are played on a diamond. Four bases form this diamond shape. The bases are 90 feet (27 m) apart. The area around the bases is called the **infield**. At the center of the infield is the pitcher's mound. The grass area beyond the bases is called the outfield. White lines start at **home plate** and go toward the outfield. These are the foul lines. Baseballs hit outside these lines are out of play. The outfield walls are about 300-450 feet (91-137 m) from home plate.

Big Days!

The Cubs have had some good seasons in their history. Here are three of them:

1907–08: A Cubs team led by great pitching won back-to-back World Series championships.

1984: Good and bad: The Cubs won the first two games of the N.L. Championship Series. One more win would send them to the World Series. Then they lost three straight to the San Diego Padres. Once again, the Cubs were disappointed.

2007–08: The Cubs made the playoffs two seasons in a row. It was the first time they had done that in 100 years. However, they lost all their games in those two playoff series.

The Cubs danced on the field after they earned the 2008 N.L. Central championship. ▶

Tough Days!

The Cubs have had a lot of tough seasons. Here are three of the worst:

1962: The Cubs lost 103 games, their worst record ever. They finished next to last in the N.L.

1945: The Billy Goat Curse bit the Cubbies! A man tried to bring a good-luck goat into a World Series game at Wrigley Field. He and the goat weren't let in. The man put a "curse" on the team. He said they would never win another World Series game. And they haven't . . .

2003: The Cubs were leading 3-0 in the eighth inning. A win would take them to the World Series. But a fan tried to grab a foul ball that would have ended the inning. The Florida Marlins won the game and then knocked the Cubs out of their chance at the Series.

◀ The fan in the blue cap kept Moises Alou from catching this foul ball. Did this play also continue the "Cubs' Curse"?

Meet the Fans

Cubs fans are the most loyal in baseball. They have to be. Their team hasn't won a title in 100 years! They pack Wrigley Field for every game. They started a baseball tradition a few seasons ago. When an opponent hits a homer into the stands . . . the fans throw it back! Cubs fans also love to watch the games from nearby rooftops.

Some Cubs fans are called "bleacher creatures." They're named after their ▶
seats above the outfield.

Ernie Banks, Shortstop/First Base

Heroes Then . . .

In the 1880s and 1890s, Chicago's Cap Anson was one of the best all-around players. He was the first player to reach 3,000 hits in a career. Star pitcher Mordecai Brown was called "Three-Finger" because he had hurt his hand in a farming accident. In 1930, Hack Wilson had 191 runs batted in (RBI). That's still the most ever in one season. In the 1950s and 1960s, Ernie Banks earned the nickname "Mr. Cub." A slugging infielder, he was loved by the fans. One of his favorite sayings was, "It's such a nice day. Let's play two!" In the 1980s, second baseman Ryne Sandberg was a **Gold Glove** fielder, a top base stealer, and a home-run slugger. In the late 1990s and early 2000s, Sammy Sosa had three seasons with 60 or more homers.

◀ Ryne "Ryno" Sandberg was one of the best-hitting second basemen ever. Inset: Ernie Banks smacked 512 home runs!

23

Heroes Now . . .

Outfielder Alfonso Soriano can do it all. He's one of only a few players to have 40 homers and 40 steals in the same season! He did it with the Texas Rangers in 2006. With the Cubs, he's been a powerhouse, too! Big first baseman Derrek Lee was the 2005 N.L. batting champ and is a fine fielder, too. At third base, Aramis Ramirez is a top young player. A hero in Japan, outfielder Kosuke Fukudome has become a fan favorite in Chicago, too. Power pitcher Carlos Zambrano has been one of the Cubs' best since 2003. The man known as "Big Z" threw a no-hitter in 2008.

Derrek Lee, First Base

Carlos Zambrano, Pitcher

Alfonso Soriano, Outfield

CATCHER'S CHEST PROTECTOR

TEAM JERSEY

UNDERSHIRT

CATCHER'S MITT

BAT

BATTING HELMET

BATTING GLOVE

TEAM PANTS

CATCHER'S SHIN GUARD

Kosuke Fukudome, Outfield

BASEBALL CLEATS

Gearing Up

Baseball players all wear a team jersey and pants. They have to wear a team hat in the field and a helmet when batting. Take a look at Geovanny Soto and Kosuke Fukudome to see some other parts of a baseball player's uniform.

THE BASEBALL

A Major League baseball weighs about 5 ounces (142 g). It is 9 inches (23 cm) around. A leather cover surrounds hundreds of feet of string. That string is wound around a small center of rubber and cork.

SPORTS STATS

Here are some all-time career records for the Chicago Cubs. All the stats are through the 2009 season.

HOME RUNS

Sammy Sosa, 545
Ernie Banks, 512

RUNS BATTED IN

Cap Anson, 1,879
Ernie Banks, 1,636

BATTING AVERAGE

Bill Madlock, .336
Riggs Stephenson, .336

WINS BY A PITCHER

Charley Root, 201

Mordecai Brown, 188

STOLEN BASES

Frank Chance, 400

Ryne Sandberg, 344

WINS BY A MANAGER

Cap Anson, 1,283

EARNED RUN AVERAGE

Mordecai Brown, 1.80

Jack Pfiester, 1.85

Glossary

Gold Glove an award given to the top fielder at each position in each league

home plate a five-sided rubber pad where batters stand to swing, and where runners touch base to score runs

infield the area around and between the four bases of a baseball diamond

loyal supporting something no matter what

manager the person who is in charge of the team and chooses who will bat and pitch

opponents teams or players that play against each other

outfield the large, grass area beyond the infield of a baseball diamond

rivals teams that play each other often and have an ongoing competition

World Series the Major League Baseball championship, played each year between the winners of the American and National Leagues

Find Out More

BOOKS

Buckley, James Jr. *Eyewitness Baseball*. New York: DK Publishing, 2010.

Stewart, Mark. *Chicago Cubs*. Chicago: Norwood House Press, 2008.

Teitelbaum, Michael. *Baseball*. Ann Arbor, MI: Cherry Lake Publishing, 2009.

WEB SITES

Visit our Web page for links about the Chicago Cubs and other pro baseball teams.

childsworld.com/links

Note to Parents, Teachers, and Librarians: We routinely verify our Web links to make sure they are safe, active sites—so encourage your readers to check them out!

Index

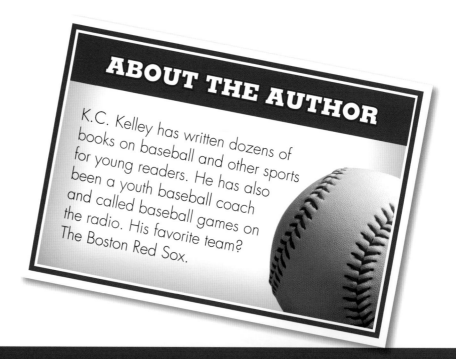

ABOUT THE AUTHOR

K.C. Kelley has written dozens of books on baseball and other sports for young readers. He has also been a youth baseball coach and called baseball games on the radio. His favorite team? The Boston Red Sox.